ACCLAIM FOR COLLEEN COBLE

"Coble's atmospheric and suspenseful series launch should appeal to fans of Tracie Peterson and other authors of Christian romantic suspense."

—*LIBRARY JOURNAL*
REVIEW OF *TIDEWATER INN*

"Romantically tense, but with just the right touch of danger, this cowboy love story is surprisingly clever—and pleasingly sweet."

—USAToday.com REVIEW
OF *BLUE MOON PROMISE*

"Colleen Coble will keep you glued to each page as she shows you the beauty of God's most primitive land and the dangers it hides."

—www.RomanceJunkies.com

"[An] outstanding, completely engaging tale that will have you on the edge of your seat . . . A must-have for all fans of romantic suspense!"

—TheRomanceReadersConnection.com
REVIEW OF *ANATHEMA*

"Colleen Coble lays an intricate trail in *Without a Trace* and draws the reader on like a hound with a scent."

—*ROMANTIC TIMES*, 4½ STARS

"Coble's historical series just keeps getting better with each entry."
—LIBRARY JOURNAL STARRED
REVIEW OF THE LIGHTKEEPER'S BALL

"Don't ever mistake [Coble's] for the fluffy romances with a little bit of suspense. She writes solid suspense, and she ties it all together beautifully with a wonderful message."
—LIFEINREVIEWBLOG.COM
REVIEW OF LONESTAR ANGEL

"This book has everything I enjoy: mystery, romance, and suspense. The characters are likable, understandable, and I can relate to them."
—THEFRIENDLYBOOKNOOK.COM

"[M]ystery, danger, and intrigue as well as romance, love, and subtle inspiration. *The Lightkeeper's Daughter* is a 'keeper.'"
—ONCEUPONAROMANCE.NET

"Colleen is a master storyteller."
—KAREN KINGSBURY,
BESTSELLING AUTHOR OF
UNLOCKED AND *LEARNING*

A
HEART'S
OBSESSION

ALSO BY COLLEEN COBLE

SUNSET COVE NOVELS
The Inn at Ocean's Edge
Mermaid Moon
(Available December 2015)

HOPE BEACH NOVELS
Tidewater Inn
Rosemary Cottage
Seagrass Pier

UNDER TEXAS STARS NOVELS
Blue Moon Promise
Safe in His Arms

THE MERCY FALLS SERIES
The Lightkeeper's Daughter
The Lightkeeper's Bride
The Lightkeeper's Ball

LONESTAR NOVELS
Lonestar Sanctuary
Lonestar Secrets
Lonestar Homecoming
Lonestar Angel
All is Calm: A Lonestar
Christmas Novella (e-book only)

THE ROCK HARBOR SERIES
Without a Trace
Beyond a Doubt
Into the Deep
Cry in the Night
Silent Night: A Rock Harbor
Christmas Novella (e-book only)

THE ALOHA REEF SERIES
Distant Echoes
Black Sands
Dangerous Depths
Midnight Sea
Holy Night: An Aloha Reef
Christmas Novella (e-book only)

Alaska Twilight
Fire Dancer
Abomination
Anathema
Butterfly Palace

NOVELLAS INCLUDED IN:
Smitten
Secretly Smitten
Smitten Book Club

OTHER NOVELLAS
Bluebonnet Bride

A
HEART'S
OBSESSION

COLLEEN COBLE

THOMAS NELSON
Since 1798

NASHVILLE   MEXICO CITY   RIO DE JANEIRO

Published in Nashville, Tennessee, by Thomas Nelson. Thomas Nelson is a registered trademark of HarperCollins Christian Publishing, Inc.

Thomas Nelson titles may be purchased in bulk for educational, business, fund-raising, or sales promotional use. For information, please e-mail SpecialMarkets@ThomasNelson.com.

Scripture quotations are from the King James Version of the Bible.

Publisher's Note: This novel is a work of fiction. Names, characters, places, and incidents are either products of the author's imagination or used fictitiously. All characters are fictional, and any similarity to people living or dead is purely coincidental.

Library of Congress Cataloging-in-Publication Data Available Upon Request.
ISBN: 978-0-7180-3165-7

Printed in the United States of America
15 16 17 18 19 RRD 6 5 4 3 2 1

In memory of my brother Randy Rhoads, who taught me to love the mountains of Wyoming, and my grandparents Everett and Eileen Everroad, who loved me unconditionally. May you walk those heavenly mountains with joy.

A Letter from the Author

D ear Reader,
　　I can't tell you how excited I am to share this story with you! It's the first series I ever wrote, and it will always be special to me because writing was how I dealt with my brother Randy's death. You'll see a piece of my dear brother in Rand's character throughout this series. These six books were originally titled *Where Leads the Heart* and *Plains of Promise*. They haven't been available in print form for nearly ten years, so I'm thrilled to share them with you. I've made

some massive changes to them, and I hope you enjoy these new, updated stories. This installment begins to show what Sarah faces in winning Rand back again.

When my brother Randy was killed in a freak lightning accident, I went to Wyoming to see where he had lived. As I stood on the parade ground at Fort Laramie, the idea for the first book dropped into my head. I went home excited to write it. It took a year to write, and I thought for sure there would be a bidding war on it! :) Not so much. It took six more years for a publisher to pick it up. But the wait was worth it!

This series seemed a good one to break up into a serialization model to introduce readers to my work. Even in my early stories, I had to have villains and danger lurking around the corner. :) I hope you enjoy this trip back in time with me.

E-mail me at colleen@colleencoble.com and let me know what you think!

Love,
Colleen

ONE

〜

The town of Wabash, Indiana, bustled with activity as the horse's hooves clopped along the plank street and up the hill. Rand Campbell reined in the mare pulling the family buckboard and stopped in front of the train depot. The engine shrieked and puffed out a billow of soot that burned his throat as he, Jacob, and Shane climbed down. Now that the time had arrived for his departure, Rand wished he had been able to

〜

stay longer. Leaving his mother and father had been rough. Ma had cried, then pressed his grandma's Bible into his hand before hurrying away, and Pa wouldn't even come out of the barn to say good-bye.

Shane snuffled, and Rand ruffled his brother's blond hair, then hugged him. "I'm counting on you to take care of the family, squirt." Though at fifteen, the lad was eye level with Rand.

Shane bit his quivering lip and nodded, straightening his shoulders. He trotted around behind the buckboard, heaved the saddle over one shoulder, then led Ranger to the waiting train. Rand's horse would accompany him west.

Rand put his hand in his pocket. His fingers rubbed against a familiar round shape. He'd smuggled it into the prison in his shoe and had spent months sanding off the engraving on the golden eagle coin before chiseling his and Sarah's names into the gold.

His gaze swept the familiar sights of Wabash at the top of the hill. The whitewashed courthouse, the jail to the west of it, and the bustle of Commercial Row just down the steep Wabash Street hill made his heart ache at the thought of leaving. But knowing he'd never see Sarah again hurt the most.

He'd come home after his internment in Andersonville Prison to find his fiancée engaged to Ben Croftner. When things were sorted out and Ben's lies were exposed, Rand had hoped Sarah would go west with him, but she'd put her family above him. He'd taken that hurt and used it to build a wall around his heart.

He fingered the love token. What good would it do in his pocket? He'd never give it to anyone else because he'd never feel like this about anyone else. That kind of love was dead for him.

He pulled out the token and thrust it into Jacob's hand. "Give this to Sarah, Jake. Tell her I'm sorry it didn't work out and I hope she has a happy life."

Jacob's fingers closed around the token. "You make it sound like there's no hope for the two of you."

"There isn't. I wish it weren't so, but I doubt I'll see Sarah again." Rand hefted the haversack over his shoulder and picked up the hamper of food, then his satchel.

"All aboard!"

He was a cavalry man, and this was what he wanted—a life he made for himself, beholden to no one. After one last look at his brothers, he raced toward the plodding train and jumped up the steep steps. He caught one last glimpse of Jacob, standing with one arm upraised, his other arm around their younger brother, Shane. Rand waved until the buckboard with the two figures beside it was no longer in view, then took a deep breath and limped to a vacant seat. His great adventure was about to begin.

Sarah Montgomery sat on a rock along the banks of the Wabash River and listened to the train whistle blow as the engine left the station. The sun on this fine September day warmed her face. A robin, its red breast a bright flash of color, fluttered by to land on a nearby gooseberry bush. The bird swooped down to grab a worm. The rhythm of life went on even though her heart felt dead in her chest. She was only nineteen, but right now she felt like ninety.

How did she go on after losing Rand and then finding him again, only to watch him leave her without a thought? Time stretched in front of her, a lifetime spent without the man she'd loved since she was a girl. A vision of his dark hair and eyes resided in her heart and always would.

She picked up the book she'd brought with her, *A Christmas Carol*. The novel absorbed her until the sun moved lower in the sky. She closed it and glanced around to make sure she had all her belongings before going back to the house to start dinner.

"Sarah?"

She looked up to see Jacob, Rand's younger brother, approaching with a tentative smile. "He's gone?"

Jacob, dressed in his blue cavalry uniform, took off his wide-brimmed hat and turned it in his hands. "I'm sorry, Sarah. How you doing?"

Though her eyes burned, she was past tears. "I'll be fine." She tipped up her chin. "I have Papa and Joel to care for." She studied the compassion in Jacob's brown eyes. "D-Did he say anything about me?"

Jacob nodded and stepped closer. He pulled his hand from his pocket, and something metallic winked in the sunlight. "He asked me to give you this."

She rose from her perch on a rock and reached out to take it from him. Her fingers rubbed over the gold metal. "A love token." She choked out the words as she stared at the words engraved in the metal. *Rand and Sarah.*

"He worked on this in prison."

Her fingers traced the engraving. "Did he say anything about me joining him?"

Jacob's eyes held sympathy as he shook his head. "No, he didn't, Sarah. I'm sorry. H-He said to tell you he was sorry it didn't work out and he hoped you'd have a happy life."

The pain crushed in on her again. The good-bye was final, just like the one that loomed with her father. Her fingers closed around the coin, and the edges bit into her palm. "Thank you, Jacob. I'll treasure it."

Kansas City was a sprawling assortment of wooden shops and storefronts. The streets teemed with horses and cattle, buggies and buckboards. And people. Everywhere, people hurried across the muddy streets and crowded the uneven boardwalks. Rand felt invigorated by the hustle and bustle, despite the smell of manure and the distant lowing of cattle from the stockyards.

A broad-shouldered man shouting orders to his cowboys pushed past Rand with a brief tip of his hat. Rand stared after him. His stint in the cavalry would give him the opportunity to find his own spread. Someday he'd bring his own cattle to a stockyard like this one.

Across from the depot was the Holladay Stagecoach station, and he walked across the street and stood in line behind another soldier. "Heading to Fort Leavenworth, then on to Fort Laramie too?"

The other man turned with a grin on his open, friendly face. "Sure am. Been on leave and kinda hate to go back. You new?"

"Lieutenant Rand Campbell." He thrust out a soot-streaked hand.

"Lieutenant Isaac Liddle." He shook Rand's proffered hand, then took off his wide-brimmed hat and wiped his forehead with a bandanna. "What unit you with?"

"H Troop, Third Cavalry. You?"

"Third Battalion. You're going to like Old Bedlam. You heard of it?"

Rand shook his head, liking the looks of his companion. Isaac reminded him in some ways of Jacob. Though Isaac had auburn hair and a dusting of freckles, he had the same muscular build and quiet, friendly manner as Jacob. Strong, capable hands. A man you could depend on. And from what he'd heard of the Indian Wars, you wanted that kind of man around.

Isaac grinned. "It's what we call the single officers' quarters. It came by its name legitimate. A lot of loud shenanigans go on at all hours. At least I assume that's where you'll be quartered. I don't see a pretty lady with you. You're not married?"

"No." He pushed away an image of Sarah's heart-shaped face, long red-gold hair, and dancing green eyes.

"I was hopin'. Fort Laramie doesn't have many women right now." He put his hat back. "Where you from?"

"Wabash, Indiana. Born and raised on a farm about two miles out of town." Rand was grateful for the change in topic. "Where you hail from?"

"El Paso, Texas." Isaac held one hand out in front of him hastily when he saw Rand's eyebrows rise. "But I fought for the Union."

That explained his accent. The line moved forward, and Rand followed. "What's the status of the Indian Wars?"

Isaac frowned. "We got trouble brewing with Red Cloud. That's why so many are being sent out for reinforcements. They haven't attacked Laramie yet, but we have to send out troops even on woodcutting duty. Maybe it's a good thing you don't have a wife. She would be an added worry."

Jacob was bringing Amelia. Rand glanced toward the telegraph station. There was no time to send a telegram to his brother, though, and even if he did, Rand didn't see Amelia agreeing to stay behind. A frown on his face, he picked up his luggage, waved to Isaac, then went to the livestock car to get Ranger for the trek to Fort Leavenworth.

Rand's brass buttons and buckles glimmered in the sunshine, and Ranger's sleek black coat shone. He and his detachment met Major DuBois about three miles north of Fort Leavenworth. There was no mistaking the major. He sat on his black horse with stiff military bearing, and his uniform was precisely brushed and neat.

Rand saluted. "Good morning, sir. I'm Lieutenant Campbell, and I'm pleased to escort you to Fort Laramie." He'd been at Fort Leavenworth a week when he was ordered to meet a column and escort them on to Fort Laramie.

The major saluted smartly. "At ease, Lieutenant."
He dismounted and motioned for Rand to do the same.
"How's the situation with the Indians? Any trouble
brewing?"

Rand dismounted and joined the major. "Nothing
I can put my finger on, sir. But I have an uneasy feeling that something's brewing that we can't see right
now. There have been grumblings about the miners
tramping through the Sioux hunting grounds on the
Bozeman Trail. Red Cloud hasn't come in for rations,
and some of our tame Oglala Sioux say he's calling for
a fight to the knife. I don't trust him."

The major waved his hand dismissively. "We'll
deal with him if he steps out of line."

The flap to the ambulance behind them opened
and a young woman stepped through the opening.
"Good morning, Daddy. Why have we stopped? Have
we arrived?"

Something about her reminded Rand of Sarah.
Maybe it was the sweet smile she directed his way or
the red in her hair. He waited to be introduced.

The major smiled. "Lieutenant, I'd like you to meet
my daughter, Jessica. And my wife, Mrs. DuBois.
Ladies, this is Lieutenant Rand Campbell. He has
come to escort us into the fort."

"Call me Letty, dear," the older woman, a softer, plumper version of the daughter, murmured as she placed her round hand in Rand's.

Rand gripped it briefly and muttered some response, but his gaze was on the major's daughter. Her fiery red hair was arranged in a mass of curls that framed her delicate face in a halo of color. She smiled at him as though he were the first man she'd ever seen.

"I'm *very* pleased to meet you," she said softly. Her silky hand lingered on his.

Rand was aware he was staring, but he couldn't seem to stop. He told the private driving the ambulance to take Ranger and he would drive the ladies into the fort. All the while he was conscious of Jessica's blue eyes fastened on him. Sarah might not have wanted to be with him, but that didn't mean other women weren't interested.

Ben Croftner's wounds had healed from the beating he'd taken at Rand Campbell's hands, but his rage still simmered. He propped his boots on the gleaming surface of his new walnut coffee table and stared across the room at his brother.

"I saw Wade Montgomery at the feed store today, Labe."

Labe looked down at his hands. "That so?"

His brother's cautious tone told him that Labe still feared Rand. "Campbell is long gone. He won't stop my plans again."

"You need to give up that obsession with Sarah." Labe's hands twisted in his lap, and he didn't look at Ben, as if fearing his response.

As well he should. Ben gritted his teeth but didn't waste the time to chide him. "Wade is still in favor of a marriage between Sarah and me. He's going to do all in his power to make it happen."

"She won't have none of it. Not after what you did."

"She took my ring. I had rights."

Labe just ducked his head again. "Has he told Sarah?"

"No, but he's going to. His father isn't long for this world. Once he's gone, Sarah won't have anyone encouraging her in her crazy ideas. She'll be with me yet."

TWO

Sarah glanced out the kitchen window at the big elm tree, brilliant with October color. Wade would be home soon for dinner, and she wanted to get the meal over with so she could escape to her room and finish her book. Reading was the only thing that kept her thoughts from yearning for what she could never have. Her fingers went to the love token hanging from a chain around her neck.

A sound made her whirl around. "Papa, you startled me." She looked at him with new eyes, seeing his frailty and the yellow tinge of his skin.

He wheezed as he lowered himself into the chair she pulled out for him at the table. She sat beside him and began to peel potatoes.

Her father leaned back in his chair and sighed. "You should have gone with Rand, you know."

Sarah nicked her finger with the knife. "I couldn't leave you!"

"You're not a little girl anymore. And there comes a time in every person's life when he has to step out and stand on his own feet. Rand was ready, and I think you are too. We both know I won't be around much longer."

Her heart squeezed at the certainty in his eyes. "No, Papa."

He held up a hand at her protest. "You just don't want to admit it, my dear girl. I would rest easier if I knew you were settled and happy. I never expected you to give up without a fight. You had to fight to get him in the first place. Remember all the tears until I let you put your hair up and wear your mother's green satin dress for Christmas dinner with the Campbells the year you turned sixteen?"

Sarah smiled at the memory. "It worked too. That was the first time he saw me as anything but a pesky younger sister. But he's five states away now. What can I do?" Tears started into her eyes, and she brushed them away angrily.

Her father stood. "I don't know the answer, but I'm sure God will tell you if you'll listen." He patted the top of her head and turned to leave the kitchen.

She rose to run water over the potatoes and heard a sound behind her. A thump and a groan. Her heart in her throat, she whirled to see her father lying on the floor. Sarah flung herself down beside him and took his hand.

"Papa, it's me," she whispered. "Don't die, please don't die. Just hold on." She screamed Joel's name, then Rachel's.

At her voice, his pale lids fluttered and his cold fingers moved under hers. She leaned closer. "Don't try to talk. I'm here with you."

Her eight-year-old brother, Joel, came rushing down the steps. His face went ashen when he saw their father on the floor. "Get the doctor," she told him before bending back to Papa. Wade's wife, eight months pregnant, waddled into the hall from the parlor. She stopped and sank to her knees on the other side of Papa.

With an effort, Papa opened his eyes again and

tried to smile. "Don't cry, my dear girl. The Lord is waiting for me, and I'm going to be with your mama at last." He blinked a few times, then focused on her face. "Just be happy, Sarah. You fight for your Rand, if you must, and don't let Wade bully you into anything." He coughed weakly. "But don't leave Joel with Wade. Promise me." His voice grew stronger and he raised his head slightly. "Promise!"

"I promise," Sarah whispered as she felt his icy fingers loosen. The breath eased from his mouth. His chest didn't rise again. "Papa!" Sarah stared at him. This couldn't be real. He'd just been talking with her. She clutched his hand tighter. "Don't leave me, Papa!" She kissed his cheek and gathered his head into her lap. "Dear God, no," she sobbed. "Don't take him. This can't be happening." She looked over at Rachel kneeling and weeping on the other side of Papa's body. "He's just unconscious, Rachel. He can't be dead."

Rachel just shook her head and cried hard. "I'm so sorry, Sarah. We all loved him. He was a good man." She scooted around and put her arm around Sarah's shaking shoulders. "He never got over missing your mama. Just be happy he's finally with her again."

"But I still need him." Sarah's voice was bewildered as she stared down into her father's peaceful face. "He can't leave me now." She touched his grizzled cheek, already cooling.

They both turned as Wade and Doc Seth rushed in the door with Joel on their heels. "Help him, Doc," Sarah pleaded as the doctor knelt beside his friend of nearly forty years and put the stethoscope to her father's chest.

There was a long pause, then the doctor straightened. "I'm sorry, Sarah. William's gone." His voice was hoarse and moisture glistened in his eyes.

The words hammered into Sarah's brain. She reached for Joel, who had begun to cry. He was hers now. She had to keep her little brother safe and the family from splintering apart.

Amelia looked radiant as she turned to let Sarah button up her wedding dress. Sarah's heart filled at the joy on her face. At least there was some good in these dark days since her father's funeral. "You look beautiful. Jacob will be tongue-tied."

"I hope so." Amelia faced her. "I'm so glad you came. I wasn't sure you'd be up to it."

"I wouldn't miss it." Through the open window,

Sarah heard the sounds of buckboards and buggies as the guests began to arrive for the ceremony. "Papa said something before he died. He told me to fight for Rand. I can't do that from here. I want to go with you and Jacob when you leave for Fort Laramie."

Amelia's eyes went wide. "I would love that! I've been so fearful of being alone when Jacob is out on patrol. Having you there would make it all bearable."

Sarah's fingers went to the token at her neck. "Will Jacob agree?"

"I'm sure he will. I'll talk to him tonight." Amelia hugged her tight. "I can't tell you how pleased I am. Now let's go get me hitched." Her smile beamed out. "We're leaving in two days. Can you be ready by then?"

"Of course." Her thoughts raced as she tried to think of all she should bring. "What about Joel? I can't leave him behind. He belongs with me."

Amelia's smile seemed less certain, but she nodded. "You can't leave Wade to raise Joel."

As soon as the wedding was over, Sarah rushed home to pack. She had to tell Joel they were leaving too. She found him in the barn forking hay into the horse stalls. He paused to wipe his face, and she realized he was crying.

Dust motes danced in the air, and she sneezed at the hay. Joel dropped the pitchfork and rushed into her arms. She held him close, not minding that he smelled of horse manure and barn dirt. "We're going to be okay, Joel. Has Wade been hard on you?" Though he was still half boy, she was beginning to catch a glimpse of the man he would be with the right influences. Being away from Wade would be better for him.

He pulled away and shrugged. "Not any more than usual."

"I have something to tell you." She could barely keep her voice at a whisper. "We're leaving with Amelia and Jacob when they go to Fort Laramie."

His green eyes, so like her own, widened, and a smile lifted the corners of his lips. "For real?"

She nodded. "I need you to pack what you'll need in one suitcase. We'll have to travel as light as we can."

His smile faded. "Wade won't let us."

"He'll have no choice." She turned toward the barn door. "I'm going to fix dinner and then pack. Don't say anything until after I tell Wade."

She hurried into the kitchen and found Rachel at the table, cutting carrots. "Any labor pangs?"

Rachel shook her head. "Not yet." She rubbed her swollen belly. "I'm so ready."

The kitchen door banged open and Wade stomped in. "Supper's not done yet?" he growled as he hung up his red plaid jacket. He turned and looked at Sarah. "There's something I want to talk to you about."

She didn't trust his mild tone. He wanted something from her, and she had a sinking feeling she knew what it was. "What about?"

"Your future." He stared at her challengingly. "I saw Ben in town the other day, and for some reason he still wants to marry you. I told him I didn't see any reason why you wouldn't. That good-for-nothing Campbell went off and left you in the lurch and—"

"No." The short, clipped word cut him off just as he was picking up steam.

"You will do what I say. You're under age and my ward." Wade compressed his lips in an effort to keep his temper.

"I will *not* marry Ben. Rand and I belong together. Papa's last words to me were to fight for Rand. I'll never marry Ben."

"Well, that's just too bad, missy. You'd better get used to the idea because you will do as I say. Campbell has run off to the frontier, and you'll never see him again anyway." He shoved her toward the door. "You'll stay in your room until you agree to abide by my decisions." He grabbed her arm and dragged her up the stairs and into her room.

Sarah stared at the closed door in disbelief as the lock clicked shut behind her brother. His behavior had shocked her so much she hadn't put up much fight. "You can't keep me in here, Wade! This isn't the Middle Ages!" She heard him going down the steps and ran to the door. "Let me out of here. I'll never marry Ben—never!" She twisted the latch to no avail, then kicked at the solid oak door in a helpless frenzy of rage.

Pain exploded in her toe, and she hobbled over to sit on the bed and think. Joel would be in the house soon. He'd let her out. But what then? What could she do? She bit her lip and turned to look around her room. She could pack in peace.

Instead of asking to be let out, Sarah spent the night planning her escape and was bleary-eyed from lack of sleep by the time morning came. She and Joel had whispered through the door until they were both ready to go. She hid her suitcase under the bed just as she heard Wade's heavy tread outside the door.

The lock turned and he stepped into the room. She wanted to throw something at him as soon as she saw his smug face. "Ready to be reasonable yet?"

"Do I have a choice?" She kept her face averted so he couldn't see her eyes.

He smiled. "I knew you'd come around. I had Rachel save you some breakfast."

The exultation in his voice caused her to clench her hands to keep from screaming at him. "I'm not hungry."

He eyed her bent head, then seemed satisfied that he'd broken her spirit and nodded. "Fine. I'll go talk to Pastor Stevens, and we'll discuss when the wedding can take place." He left the door open behind him and tromped back downstairs and out the door.

Sarah sprang to her feet as soon as the buggy rumbled down the rutted track toward town. Feverishly she pulled her suitcase from under her bed. As she picked it up and turned toward the door, she heard someone in the hall. She froze until she realized it was just Joel.

His red hair didn't look as though it had been combed for days, but his eyes held more excitement than she'd seen in ages. "I've got my suitcase ready."

"Go get it, and I'll meet you downstairs."

"Can I take my rifle?"

Sarah hesitated as she looked into his pleading face. The less baggage the better, but the rifle had been Papa's and she didn't have the heart to make him leave it behind. She nodded, and he slung it over his shoulder and picked up his suitcase. They slipped down the steps and came face-to-face with Rachel.

She looked from the suitcases to Sarah's face. "You're leaving. I knew Wade would never force you to fall in with his plans—but who has ever been able to tell him anything?" She pushed her brown hair back from her forehead and held out her arms.

Sarah put down her suitcase and went to Rachel with a sigh. "I'll miss you, Rachel. But I have to find Rand." Her words were muffled against Rachel's shoulder. She drew away and looked into her sister-in-law's eyes. "Don't tell Wade I've gone."

Rachel smiled faintly. "He won't be back till suppertime. If you hurry, you can catch the afternoon train and be long gone before he knows you've left." She hugged her fiercely, then shoved her toward the door. "Write when you get there. And don't forget about me and the baby. We love you."

Sarah gulped and wiped her eyes. "I know, Rachel. And you've been a real sister to me. Make sure you write us when the baby's born."

Rachel nodded, then smiled through her tears and made a shooing motion with her apron. "You'd best get going. You have a lot to get done today."

Joel hurried ahead to hitch up the wagon while Sarah took one last look at the home where she'd been born. The sun shone through the bare trees in dappled patterns on the front porch roof. The solid two-story seemed so safe and familiar. She could see the red barn just behind it where she'd played in the haymow as a child. The chicken coop off to the east, the pasture beyond that, and all around the gently rolling hills of Montgomery land. It was all so heart-breakingly beloved.

She'd never had any plans of leaving her home. At least not any farther than the knoll beyond the pasture. Would she ever see it again? And who would tend Papa's grave?

She choked back tears and climbed up beside Joel. This was no time for tears, for second thoughts. Wade had left her no choice. She waved one last good-bye at Rachel, then stared firmly ahead.

THREE

Sarah stared out the window of the stagecoach as the barren landscape swept by. The train portion of the trip had been much more pleasant. The stagecoach reeked of dusty leather, hair tonic, horse, and underlying everything else, the unlovely aroma of unwashed bodies. They'd lurched along for ten days already. Occasionally, several of the soldiers traveling with them tried to strike up a conversation, but they soon fell silent under Jacob's glowering.

The frozen landscape rolled past all that day and

through the night. The next morning was colder, and a hint of moisture was in the blustery wind. The soldiers predicted a blizzard but not until the next day. They should all be safe and snug in Fort Laramie by then.

Sarah sighed, and her breath steamed. "I hope I get a chance to bathe before I see Rand. I must look terrible." She could feel her hair hanging in straggly wisps against her cheeks. The last time she pushed it out of her face, her gloves had come away smeared with dirt. Rand would take one look at her and send her home.

Jacob shuffled his feet on the other side of Amelia as the driver gave a shout from topside. He grinned at Sarah. "Sounds like we're there."

Sarah moaned and tried to pat the strands of hair back into some semblance of order as she lifted the leather covering and peered out the window at the fort. Surrounded by rocky soil and sagebrush, it sprawled across the Laramie River, and its frame and adobe buildings lined a wide parade ground fortified with mountain howitzers. But it was all so barren. The fort seemed a tiny oasis in a vast plain of frigid wasteland.

She gave an involuntary gasp when she saw the Indians encamped all around the fort, their teepees gleaming in the sunshine. Hundreds of them. Women squatted around open fires, and children shouted and played in the dust.

"Has the fort been overrun? Is it safe to disembark?"

The garrulous old soldier across the aisle chuckled. "Fort Laramie's the headquarters for the Sioux. There's always a passel of Sioux 'round here. You'll git used to it." He nodded to her. "The name's Rooster, miss."

"But there's no stockade." She shuddered. "What if they turn hostile?"

"There's always plenty of hostiles around, but they know better than to attack a fort as well garrisoned as this one. You don't need to worry none, missy. The most them savages ever done was run howling through the pasture to stampede the horses."

Several soldiers manned a ferry, and the stagecoach rolled onto the vessel. Out on the river, the wind cut through Sarah's clothing. The soldiers guided the stagecoach horses off the ferry and onto the road, then stepped back. Sarah's heart pounded as the horses pulled the stage up the hill and it rolled to a stop. The driver threw open the door and helped the two ladies down before climbing on top and tossing the luggage down to the eager hands waiting below.

Sarah stared all around in dismay. It was not at

all as she'd imagined. The adobe buildings lining the parade ground looked cheerless and unwelcoming. A U.S. flag whipped forlornly in the wind atop a flagpole on the far side of the parade ground. The fort seemed to be stuck out in the middle of nowhere with the wilderness all around. Most of the soldiers milling around stopped and stared at her and Amelia.

"It'll look better come spring," Rooster consoled.

Jacob piled their luggage together in a heap, then addressed a nearby soldier. "Could you tell me where we might find Lieutenant Rand Campbell?"

"Well don't this beat the Dutch." The soldier had a friendly, smiling face. "You've gotta be Jacob. You look enough like your brother to be two peas out of the same pod." The soldier stuck out a large calloused hand. "Isaac Liddle's my name, and Rand's my bunky."

Jacob shook his hand vigorously. "Mighty glad to meet you. Got any idea where that rascal brother of mine is?"

"Probably at mess. Bugle sounded a few minutes ago. I was headed there myself. Just follow me."

Shivering as much from nerves as from the cold, Sarah took Joel's hand and trailed behind Jacob and Amelia. She could hear shouts of laughter emanating from the officers' mess hall, and her stomach rumbled as the wind brought a mouthwatering aroma of stew to her nose.

She allowed herself a moment to imagine Rand's delight when he saw her. His dark brown eyes would light with love and surprise, and he'd rush to fold her in his arms. She could almost feel his heart thudding under her cheek now. It was all she could do not to break out in a smile.

The room was brightly lit with dozens of lanterns, and the general feeling of high spirits and fellowship warmed her as much as the heat rolling from the pot-bellied stove in the center of the room. She scanned the room quickly as their presence caused the babble of voices to soften, then still. She caught sight of Rand sitting at the far table next to two women. His handsome, square-jawed face was tanned and healthy.

Her first impulse was to call out his name and run to him, but the expression on his face as he gazed at the young redheaded woman stopped her. Sarah didn't like the dazed smile on his face or the possessive hand the woman had on his arm.

She gulped as he looked up and saw them. "Rand." She managed a tremulous smile.

He rose to his feet as the small party neared. "I didn't expect you for at least another week or two." He grabbed his brother's hand and pumped it, then hugged Amelia and Joel but didn't touch Sarah. "Hello, Sarah, Joel."

"Who are all these folks, Rand?" The woman stood and slid her hand into the crook of Rand's arm. Her perfume, some exotic flowery scent, mingled with the scent of stew. "Introduce me to your friends."

He hesitated and didn't meet Sarah's gaze. "Jessica, this is my brother Jacob; his wife, Amelia; a-and some friends from back home, Sarah Montgomery and her brother Joel."

"Pleased to meet you all." She turned a bright smile toward Jacob. "I've heard all about you, Jacob. Rand tells me you're the county boxing champion." Her smile deepened into a dimple. "I'm Jessica DuBois, and this is my mother, Mrs. Major DuBois."

The address sounded strange to Sarah, but that was how wives were addressed in the army. Jessica had aqua eyes and deep red hair that shimmered in the candlelight. Her skin was almost translucent, with a pale peach tint to her high cheekbones and full lips. Jessica's mother was a blurred image of her daughter with softer, plumper lines and a gentle expression.

"Please call me Letty, dear. Everyone does." She smiled at Amelia and Sarah. "I'm so glad to have two other women here at Laramie. We must get together for tea tomorrow. We ladies have to stick together. It helps the time go by. And you all are here just in time to help plan the wedding."

"Wedding?" Sarah looked at Rand. "Whose wedding?"

"Why, mine and Rand's, of course." Jessica hit Rand on the arm with her fan. "Why, you bad boy, haven't you told your family about us yet?"

"They had probably left Wabash by the time my letter got there," Rand said, his eyes on Sarah's face.

Sarah felt as though she were falling. She couldn't catch her breath. How could he? How could he come out and get engaged in less than two months? She fought down the tight tears in her throat as she gripped Amelia's hand. She didn't want to give the other woman the satisfaction of seeing her cry. Did she know Sarah had once been engaged to Rand?

"Congratulations," Jacob said after an awkward pause. "I had no idea you were seeing anyone."

"Rand, our journey has been long. I think we all need a place to rest and recover," Sarah said through tight lips. "Could you see about finding us a place to stay tonight?"

She just wanted to find a private corner where she could come to grips with this new reality—so very different from what she'd expected. Her face felt stiff, and if she relaxed her guard she'd fall apart.

"The quartermaster is by the door. Come with me, Jacob, and we'll get you all fixed up."

Joel tugged on Sarah's arm. "How can Rand marry that lady when he's going to marry you?"

Jessica choked on her coffee. "Why, whatever does the boy mean?"

Sarah's face burned and she wanted to run away, but she lifted her chin, determined to preserve her dignity if she could. "Rand and I were engaged before the war. Rand and I have been friends all our lives."

Jessica bit her lip and looked at her mother. "I see."

Sarah forced a smile. "If Rand is happy, I'm happy. I want to be friends with you too." She could sense Amelia's silent approval of her soft answer.

"Well, um, that's fine then," Jessica finally muttered as Jacob hurried back over to them.

"We're all fixed up," Jacob announced. "Let's go get settled. Rand will bring us over some stew after we get cleaned up."

Sarah felt numb as she held on to her skirts and

followed the little party across the windy parade
ground. How could all her hopes and dreams end like
this? What could she do?

Rand led them to an adobe building. "Captain
Leeks lives on the other side with his family, but his
family never stays here in the winter. His wife and two
sons will be back in May."

He opened the door and led them into a narrow hall
that opened onto a small, cheerless parlor. The room was
cold and barren with plain plank floors. It smelled musty
from disuse but had a lingering odor of smoke and soot.
Sarah glanced around. At least they wouldn't sleep on
the ground tonight, and they were out of the wind.

Rand knelt at the fireplace and poked at the logs.
"I'll have it warmed up in no time." He got the fire
going, then stood. "I'll leave you to get cleaned up. I'll
be back in about an hour with some supper for you."
He grinned. "Cooky likes me. When he hears we have
two new ladies, he'll be glad to whip up something."

"You're hardly limping at all now," Jacob said.

"Horse riding and walking has strengthened my
leg a lot." He turned toward the door.

When he started toward the door, Sarah stepped
into his path. She laid her hand on his arm, and the

muscles in his forearm flexed under her fingers. "We need to talk."

Rand stared down at her and swallowed. "I'll be back later. We'll talk then."

"Now, please."

Rand sighed and ran his hand through his hair. "Sarah, you need to unpack and get settled in. And we need to talk in private."

He was right. What was there to explain? It was pretty self-explanatory. No wonder he wasn't eager to discuss it with her. Was this the same man she'd known all her life? She stepped out of his way and watched him pull the door shut behind him.

Amelia touched her shoulder. "Are you all right?"

Sarah's eyes burned, but she refused to let the tears fall. She had to be strong for Joel's sake. He'd been through too much, and she couldn't let him sense her despair.

She swallowed. "I'll be all right. I just need a bit of time to adjust."

In the tiny kitchen there was a Sibley stove that Jacob soon had blazing. The warmth crept into the room and seeped into Sarah's cold skin, but nothing could reach her icy heart. A battered kettle sat on the stove. She rinsed it with water from the bucket a private brought to the back door. First they'd have a cup of tea and then see to bathing the road dust off their sore bodies. She felt as though the fine yellow grit was in every pore of her body. She could even taste its gritty presence. She looked around the small quarters. Only one bedroom opened off the kitchen. Where could they all sleep?

"I'll bring over a couple more bunks," Jacob said. "We can put one in the parlor and use it for a sofa during the day. You can sleep there, Sarah. I'll put another one in the entry for Joel, and everyone will have a little privacy. Just for tonight, you and Amelia can sleep in the bedroom, and Joel and I will put up in the barracks." He hauled the hip bath down off its peg on the wall and set it in the small bedroom. He stuck his head out the door and asked a private to go down to the river and haul some water for bathing.

Even with several kettles of boiling water added, the bathwater was barely tepid, so Sarah bathed quickly. She was ravenous by the time Rand brought over a steaming kettle of stew and bread. They wolfed down their supper in ten minutes.

Jacob yawned. "I'm beat. I think the rest of us will

turn in. Good night, honey." He kissed Amelia, then gestured for Joel to join them. The door lock snicked shut behind them.

Amelia stood. "Good night. Don't be too late, Sarah. I know you're exhausted." She sent a stern glance Rand's way before stepping to the bedroom and closing the door.

The silence stretched between them. Sarah pleated the folds of her skirt and couldn't look at Rand.

He rose and paced to the window. "I never thought I'd see you again."

"So it appears." She forced the words out of her tight throat. "I came out to keep Amelia company." She couldn't bear for him to know she'd come here expecting a much different reception. "I didn't expect to find you engaged so quickly though."

Rand raked a hand through his brown hair and his lips flattened. "I know it looks bad, Sarah, but I had a lot of time to think these past few months. I like army life. The adventure, the sense of doing something worthwhile. Something that affects other people besides just my family. I want to be part of taming the West for my country."

Sarah stared up at him. "What about your family

back in Wabash? You sound as if you never intend to go home." Though he'd said as much back in Wabash, she'd been sure he hadn't meant it, not really.

"Tell me honestly, does the thought of living in the wilderness appeal to you? You were quick to let me go alone." He knelt beside her chair. "Please try to understand."

She inhaled his manly scent mixed with the pungent odor of wood smoke, then reached out and touched his cheek, rough with stubble under her fingers. Heat flared between them before he rocked back on his heels and stood. "All I want is for you to be happy."

Hurt flashed in his eyes. "I never dreamed you'd follow me, Sarah," he said hoarsely. "If I'd even suspected it . . ." His voice trailed off. "I've made a commitment to Jessica now. She'll make an excellent army wife. She's lived in frontier forts most of her life. It hurt when you didn't love me enough to leave your family for me. Jessica will go wherever I'm sent without a complaint. She understands soldiers and their duties."

Rand turned his back to her and paced to the window. A bugle sounded in the distance. "She was here when I was hurting over your rejection. She let me know right off how she felt." He wheeled around to face her again. "What are you doing here, anyway? You said you wouldn't leave your father."

"Papa's dead." She touched his arm as she saw the hurt and shock register on his face, feelings that mirrored her own. "His heart just . . . gave out."

"Oh, Sarah." He ran a hand through his thick hair. "I really loved your pa. He was like a father to me."

"He loved you too," she said softly. "He spoke of you just before he died."

"He did?"

She nodded. "He was gone just a few minutes after we'd talked. He told me—" She broke off and bit her lip.

"He told you what?"

"It's not important now. But I didn't want Amelia to be alone."

Rand's mouth tightened. "Is that why you're here? Now that your father is gone and you don't have anything else to do, you came out here? It had nothing to do with me?"

Sarah looked down. "Do you love Jessica?" Her face felt so stiff she could barely move her lips. She had to know the answer, but her heart pounded.

"Not like I loved you. But she's been good to me.

She's very sweet and kind. I can't just throw her off like a busted saddle. I gave her my word."

Sarah stared at him. "We said good-bye before you left. Nothing has really changed." Tears burning her eyes, she stood and opened the door.

FOUR

—————————— ⚏ ——————————

What do you mean she's gone?" Ben kicked at Wade's hound that had come nosing from under the porch of the Montgomery house. "Where is she?"

The wind lifted Wade's hair. "Off to find Campbell, I would guess. I checked at the train station, and she and Joel left with Jacob and Amelia." He opened the door. "Let's get out of the wind."

Ben followed him into the parlor where a crackling fire radiated warmth into the room. He held

—————————— ⚏ ——————————

his hands at the blaze before turning to face Wade. "You let this happen. You said she'd do what you told her."

Wade dropped onto the horsehair sofa. "This is not my fault. You were the one who lied to her. She puts a lot of stock in honesty."

A thin cry echoed from upstairs. "That your kid?"

Wade nodded. "A boy. Sarah never even stayed to make sure Rachel delivered. I'm washing my hands of her. She can have whatever wretched life she wants with Campbell."

Ben could imagine the tender scene, and hatred soured his belly. "He won't keep her. A woman like Sarah needs a firm hand."

"She's always been besotted with him. I should have known it was a losing battle."

"I never lose." Ben shoved his hands in his pockets. "I'm going after her."

A plan began to form. He had connections in Washington, and while he'd never thought to go West, there were many opportunities for a clever man to become rich off the Indian Wars.

Rand was already awake when reveille sounded at five. Jacob and Joel were sleepily pulling on their overalls and boots when he strode into the bunk room to check on them. "Hurry up or you'll miss the cold slop we call breakfast."

"How's the Indian situation?" Jacob poured icy water out of a battered tin pitcher into a chipped bowl and splashed his eyes, bleary from lack of sleep.

A group of soldiers had been up playing cards all night, and their loud talk and laughter had made sleep difficult, especially with Sarah's words still running through Rand's head. Most of them had already cleared out of the long room lined with bunks, but the odor of hair tonic and dirty socks still lingered.

Rand handed his brother the cleanest towel he could find. "Bad. And likely to get worse. The Bureau of Indian Affairs has really botched things. Every agent they've sent sets out to line his pockets with what belongs to the Indians. Once one gets rich enough, he goes back east and another comes to start the same process all over again." Rand shook his head. "And it's really explosive up in the Powder River area. Quite a few miners have been killed trying to get to the gold fields."

"Much hostility around here?"

"Not really. A few skirmishes. There's mostly tame Oglala Sioux and friendly Brulé. Most of the wild Oglala are with Red Cloud at Powder River."

"The girls will be relieved to hear that."

"I was just about to check on them." Rand paused.

The smell of impending snow freshened the air and the wind stung their cheeks as they hurried across the parade ground toward the light spilling out the front window of the house. It looked warm and welcoming in the somber darkness of the predawn morning. Their breath made frosty plumes in the air, and their boots crunched against the frozen ground as they waved and called morning greetings to the soldiers heading toward the mess hall, most of them shrouded in buffalo robes against the cold. The trumpet's call to breakfast carried clearly in the clear air.

⸎

Sarah's heart was heavy as she dropped her dress over her bustle. The pagoda sleeves were quite fashionable, and at least she could hold her head up in Jessica's presence. She added a tatted collar and her favorite brooch, a rose filigree Rand had given her, then took her hairpins and went to find Amelia in the kitchen.

Rand and Jacob should be here anytime, and she wanted a moment with him. She wasn't sure what she should do. She couldn't go back home. The journey had been so arduous, she couldn't bear to think of making it again. And besides, she refused to be under Wade's thumb again. Having been his virtual prisoner had soured her against him.

She turned as she heard the men thump up the porch steps and ran to unlock the door. "Good morning." Her gaze went to Rand.

He didn't look at her. "Breakfast will be over if you two don't hurry up."

"We're almost ready. Let me finish my hair. Jacob, why don't you take Amelia and Joel and go on ahead?" Sarah's words were mumbled through a mouthful of hairpins, and she began to wind her braids up at the base of her head. With an understanding glance, Amelia adjusted her bonnet, then drew on her navy cape and followed Jacob and Joel out the door.

Sarah finished her hair with a few quick thrusts of well-placed hairpins, then looked up at Rand. "Is my being here going to be a problem for you?"

He looked away and swallowed hard. "Of course not. We'll always be friends."

She'd thought they were so much more. "I don't want to cause you any trouble."

He shrugged. "You can stay here with Jacob and Amelia. And if you want one, you won't have any trouble finding a beau. It's so rare for the men to see any unattached women—you'll probably have a dozen proposals before the week is over."

Stung by his words, Sarah tossed her head back. "I don't give my affections as easily as some."

Hurt flashed in his eyes before his expression grew guarded. "Jacob said he'd probably be sent to one of the northern forts come late spring or early summer, so I reckon we can be civil to one another for a few months."

He picked up her cloak from the foot of the bed and held it out to her courteously. She let its warmth enfold her before swishing away from him without another word. The wind struck her as she stepped onto the porch, and as she staggered, Rand caught her arm and steadied her. She was very conscious of his strong, warm fingers pressing against her arm through her cape.

His brown eyes were impersonal as he gazed down

on her. "The wind is ferocious out here. Watch your step." He led her across the parade ground toward the mess hall, the soft glow of lamplight shining out its windows and a lazy curl of smoke rising from its chimney.

With an effort, Sarah controlled her hurt and anger. She forced a smile and laid a hand on his arm before stepping into the mess hall.

It was a big open room filled with long wooden tables that seated eight to ten men. The tables closest to the stove in the center of the room were all filled.

"Rand!" Jessica, clad in a green dress, was seated across the table from Jacob, Amelia, and Joel at the table closest to the stove. She waved to them.

The other woman's shining red hair was elegantly piled high on her head, and her pale complexion was flawless. Her mother had the same cool loveliness. Sarah wanted to like her, wanted to believe Rand had made a good choice.

She smiled at her. "Good morning, Miss DuBois. You look lovely this morning. I like your dress."

Jessica smiled and the hostility in her eyes faded. "I hope you rested well, Miss Montgomery."

"I did, yes. And please, call me Sarah."

Jessica nodded, then looked up to Rand. "Don't

forget the new play at Bedlam is tonight. You did say you'd pick me up at seven, right?"

Rand nodded, and Sarah clenched her fists in the folds of her skirt until she could breathe past the pain.

"You must come, Miss Montgomery. You and your friends." Mrs. DuBois fluttered her plump, white hands. "My husband has the lead role, and you'll be able to meet all the officers."

"Please call me Sarah," she said automatically, her gaze on Rand and Jessica.

"It will be so pleasant to have other ladies at the fort." Letty shuddered delicately. "One gets so lonesome for the refined company of other women in this primitive place. Perhaps we can get together for tea tomorrow?"

Sarah forced herself to smile and accept Letty's invitation as she strained to listen to Jessica's monopoly of Rand's conversation. Obviously, he had spent considerable time with this woman and enjoyed her company. Did Rand really love her? Sarah swallowed hard. She'd accept whatever she had to.

The breakfast lasted an interminable amount of time as they ate the nearly cold flapjacks and grits and washed it all down with strong, hot coffee. Nearly every officer in the place found some excuse to stop at their table for an introduction. Jacob glowered at the attention Amelia received, but Rand just looked on impassively as the younger officers flirted with Sarah and paid her extravagant compliments.

After breakfast the quartermaster gave them rough woolen blankets, a couple of crude wooden beds with straw mattresses, and a water bucket. Amelia had brought a trunk packed with kitchen utensils and plates as well as some bright calico and gingham material, several sets of muslin sheets, and some quilts she'd made over the years.

"You're so well prepared," Sarah said. "Look at my meager belongings. I have to throw myself on your mercy."

Amelia smiled. "I've been preparing for this for a year. Anything I own is yours, and you know it."

As they carried their booty back to their quarters, Sarah was able to take a good look at their new home. Darkness had fallen so quickly last night, she hadn't really noticed much about it. A front porch ran the width of the house with wide front steps. Two doors opened off the unpainted porch.

Rand opened the main door, and they stepped inside the wide, bare entry hall. The first door led to the tiny sitting room that looked out on the front porch.

Sarah stood gazing around with her hands on her hips. There were definite possibilities. She walked through the narrow door in the small kitchen and surveyed the Sibley stove in the middle of the tiny room. There was just enough space in the corner for a small table. Hooks could be hung from the low roof for pots, and a small corner cupboard could be built in the adjoining parlor.

She turned to catch an expression of dismay on her friend's face. "What do you think, Amelia?"

Amelia brushed a stray wisp of dark hair out of her eyes. "I don't know where to begin. You take charge, Sarah. You're so much better at decisions than I am."

By midafternoon the tiny rooms had been scrubbed, Jacob had tacked the wool blankets to the floor in the sitting room and bedroom, fires blazed in all three fireplaces, and the beds were set up and ready for occupancy. Sarah and Amelia each had a lapful of material as they stitched curtains for the windows and cloths to cover the crates that would suffice as tables. Sarah could hear the thunk of axes behind the house where Joel and Jacob were chopping more wood. Isaac had told them to let the wood detail bring them more logs, but Jacob insisted he needed the exercise after the cramped stagecoach journey.

She glanced around the room in satisfaction as she sewed. They could write and ask Rachel to send a rug for the sitting room. With a few trinkets and pictures, it would be quite homey. At least it was beginning to feel like home.

50

FIVE

The bustling of the fort awakening for a new day surrounded the small quarters. Sarah yawned and slipped out of bed to peek out the window, wincing as her feet hit the icy floor. The sun glowed as it began to peek out of the eastern hills. The wind still whistled through the eaves, but the snow had stopped.

Her sense of anticipation faded when she remembered today's plans. She and Amelia had promised Mrs. DuBois they'd come to lunch at eleven. The last thing she wanted was to hear details about the wedding. And Jessica was cruel enough to delight in seeing if she could make Sarah squirm. She pressed her lips together and turned to survey her wardrobe. She'd be cool and calm. No matter what Jessica said or how much it hurt, she wouldn't let her see her pain.

By the time Amelia and Jacob opened their bedroom door, Sarah had already gone through her trunk and decided on a dress. It was a deep-green poplin trimmed with black velvet and edged with lace. A sleeveless jacket of black corded silk went over the dress and cinched over her tiny waist. Her father had bought it for her from an elegant shop in Indianapolis just six months before he died. An intricate design of velvet ribbon adorned the skirt and sleeves. Sarah had always loved the dress.

"Good morning," she called to Amelia and Jacob. She tested the curling tongs on the kitchen stove with a wet finger. It sizzled. Good. Almost hot enough.

"You're up early." Amelia yawned. "What's the occasion?"

"Have you forgotten we have a date for lunch?"

Amelia eyed her uncertainly. "You seem almost pleased. I thought you were dreading it." She put a skillet on the stove and turned to mix up a batch of biscuits.

"Don't bother with breakfast for me," Jacob interrupted. "I'm running late. I'll grab something at officers' mess." He kissed Amelia and grabbed his coat off the hook by the stove.

"Be careful," Amelia called before turning her attention back to Sarah.

"I was really hating the thought of having to be nice to Jessica, but then I decided it would just be a challenge. There must be some good in her or Rand wouldn't care about her."

Amelia smiled. "I wish you luck finding it. I haven't seen it yet."

"My, that doesn't sound like you. I've never known you to have a bad word to say about anyone but Ben. You're always telling me to have more patience with people."

Amelia's cheeks flooded with pink. "I know I shouldn't feel that way, but she makes me uneasy just as Ben did."

"Well, she's not married to Rand yet. Papa told me to fight for him." She swallowed at the thought of her father. "Could you help me with my hair? I want to look my best."

Amelia nodded and the girls spent the next hour

curling Sarah's glistening red-gold locks. They pulled her heavy hair back from her face and let the back cascade down in tight curls. After pulling a few curls forward by her ears, Sarah was finally satisfied.

Amelia looked pretty and demure in a deep blue silk dress with a lace collar and lace around the sleeves. Her dark hair was pulled back in a loose knot at the nape of her neck with a few loose curls escaping at the sides.

Sarah threw her best cloak of brown wool with bands of velvet fringe over her shoulder, tied on her green silk bonnet, and walked toward the door with Amelia in tow. Knowing she looked her best helped calm her agitation.

But when Mrs. DuBois opened the door and Sarah saw Jessica standing behind her, she felt dowdy and plain. Jessica wore a lilac-colored silk dress with an intricate pattern in the skirt. Rows of lace ruffles cascaded over the skirt and sleeves, and her lovely white shoulders were bare. Her hair was braided and looped in an intricate way Sarah had never seen. The style accentuated Jessica's high cheekbones and big blue eyes.

But Mrs. DuBois was easy to like in spite of her daughter. "Come in, come in, my dears." She fluttered her plump hands as she drew them inside the warm hallway. "We've been so looking forward to this, haven't we, Jessica dear?"

"I certainly have."

Sarah thought she detected the hint of a sneer in Jessica's smooth voice. Sarah squared her shoulders as she handed her cloak and bonnet to Mrs. DuBois.

Jessica led the way into their cheerily decorated quarters. Since Major DuBois was a senior officer, he received more deluxe accommodations than a lowly lieutenant. The parlor was large with a soft flowered carpet on the wood floor. Dainty tables and a horsehair sofa and three chairs furnished the room. Garden pictures and gold sconces adorned two walls while the fireplace dominated the third. Sarah could see the dining room through the arched doorway. A fine walnut table and chairs on another beautiful carpet occupied the center of the room. A young, attractive black woman hovered near the table.

"Rose, please pour our guests some tea," Mrs. DuBois called. "Sit down, ladies, please. I've been so looking forward to getting to know one another a little better."

Sarah sat on the sofa, expecting Amelia to sit next to her, but Jessica quickly settled there. With a glance at Sarah, Amelia sat on one of the chairs while Mrs. DuBois took possession of another one.

"What do you think of Fort Laramie so far? Are you ready to return to Indiana?" Mrs. DuBois asked.

"It's much more primitive than I expected," Sarah admitted. "And so cold. It seems very isolated."

"It's really very jolly in the summer. More ladies are here, and we have dances and parties almost every night. Wait until then before you decide to leave us."

"They'll be gone by then, Mother. Won't you?" Jessica addressed her last remark to Sarah.

Sarah forced herself to smile. "Who really knows with the army? We're hoping to stay near Rand as long as we can." She heard Jessica's sharp intake of breath.

"Excuse me for a moment, ladies," Mrs. DuBois said, seemingly unaware of the awkward pause. "I just want to peek in to see how our lunch is coming." She scurried away and disappeared behind the door on the far side of the dining room.

As soon as her mother was gone, Jessica glared at Sarah. "Just what did you mean by that remark? I've already warned you not to meddle. Nothing is going to stop this wedding. You try and I promise you, you'll be very, very sorry."

"I didn't mean anything other than we all love Rand and want to be with him as long as we can. He was gone three years and only home a few days before coming out here." Sarah looked into Jessica's eyes. "I won't lie to you and tell you I don't still love him. But I want him to be happy, and if that means marriage to you, I'll try to accept that."

Jessica's face whitened as her mother came back into the room. The look she cast at Sarah was full of venom, and Sarah could see the effort it took for her to control herself in her mother's presence.

The next hour was spent in light conversation over a delicious tea of dainty chicken salad sandwiches, tiny cakes, and cookies. The entire time Jessica's anger seethed just under her smooth surface.

"Do come again," Mrs. DuBois urged as she handed them their cloaks and bonnets. "I so enjoyed your company."

After promising they would come again, Amelia and Sarah made their escape. Amelia let out a sigh as soon as the door closed and they stepped down onto the path back home. "You've made a real enemy, Sarah. Jessica seems capable of anything."

Sarah sighed. "I meant to try to be on friendly

terms with her. I really want Rand to be happy." Tears sparkled on her lashes. "Watching him marry Jessica will be the hardest thing I've ever done, though."

They reached their door and Joel came tearing out.

Sarah caught him as he tried to rush past them. "Whoa. What's going on?" Before Joel could answer, Rand strolled out behind him.

"We're going ice fishing," Rand said. "With your permission, of course. I was going to ask before I took him, but I wasn't sure where you were, and he assured me you wouldn't mind."

"No, of course I don't mind. And we were at the DuBois's for tea," she added as he turned to go.

He stopped and gave her a quick look. "I see," was all he said. He cleared his throat. "Well, we'll be going now. He'll be back in time for supper."

"Have fun." Her heart ached as she watched him match his stride to Joel's shorter one. Her brother looked up at him adoringly as they walked away. Would things ever be right? Was it even possible to untangle this mess? She sighed and followed Amelia into the house.

Rand rapped at Colonel Maynadier's door.

"Enter."

He stepped inside the room, taking in the piles of papers scattered over the old wooden desk before saluting smartly. "You wanted to see me, sir?"

"Ah yes, Lieutenant Campbell." The colonel looked up from his scrutiny of the document in front of him. He was a tall, spare man somewhere in his forties with blond, thinning hair and pale eyebrows. But there was nothing nondescript about his eyes. They were gray and eagle sharp. The soldiers under his command knew those eyes missed nothing that concerned the well-being of Fort Laramie. Rand sometimes thought the colonel could see inside his soul with those eyes. "Camp rumor has it that a certain Lieutenant Jacob Campbell is your brother and that he arrived a few days ago with a wife and her companion. Is that correct?"

"Yes, sir."

"Excellent. I have a proposition for you. Big Ribs and some of the other chiefs have asked for their children to be instructed in the basics of a white education. Learning English, a little reading and writing. I would like to request that Miss—" He peered at the paper in front of him. "That Miss Montgomery take over the task while she is here. Lieutenant Liddle informs me that she is a most gifted, intelligent young woman and not likely to be frightened by the Indian children."

Rand swallowed his dismay. "I'll ask her, sir." The last thing he wanted was to get Sarah even more entangled in life at Fort Laramie.

He kept his face impassive as the colonel outlined his plan for the school. He'd had a hard time keeping his emotions under control the last few evenings as the five of them had curled up on the floor beside the fireplace and played checkers after he and Joel had returned from their fishing expedition. She laughed and teased like the Sarah he'd loved so long and so well. The last few evenings had been pure torture. How long must he endure her presence? He'd decided to turn his life in a new direction, and he would stick with it.

"One other thing," Colonel Maynadier said as Rand saluted and turned to go. "There's a new authorized fur trader to the Sioux downriver. Please check in on him this afternoon and see that he understands the rules governing Indian trade."

"Yes, sir." Another fur trader was the least of his worries, he fumed as he strode across the snow-covered parade ground. They were all alike anyway. All set on feathering their own nests at the expense of the Indians. They forced the Indians to pay for their own annuities with furs and made exorbitant profits when they sold the furs back east.

Sarah opened the door at his knock. Amelia was dressing in the bedroom and Jacob had already left for his duties.

Sarah's eyes darkened when he repeated the colonel's request. "When does he want me to start?"

"Right away. You're to use the chapel for now, and next spring the colonel plans to build a small schoolhouse. You'll have to improvise, though. There are no schoolbooks here and probably won't be for months." He stared at her downcast gaze. "You don't want to do it?"

She looked up then. "I'd like to help out, but I've never taught before. Teaching children who don't even know English very well sounds very difficult."

"Some of the teenagers will speak pretty well, and they'll help you with the younger ones."

She didn't look convinced. "I can try if you want me to."

"Can I go too?" Joel asked.

Sarah's brows winged up. "You actually *want* to learn something?"

Joel looked down at the floor. "There aren't any other boys to play with. I thought maybe I could teach some of them how to play baseball."

Sarah's face softened and she nodded. "We need to get on with your studies too." She turned back to Rand. "Could you find me some slate? Or some paper to lay across boards?"

"There's plenty of slate in the cliffs across the river. I'll fetch some this afternoon. I have to go that direction anyway to check on a new fur trader."

Was that tenderness in his face? It was probably just wishful thinking.

SIX

The sun shone coldly on the glistening snow as Rand threaded his way through the massive snowdrifts along the rocky trail that led downriver to the trader's establishment. He was cold through and through by the time he reached the group of small buildings bustling with activity. The pure snow had been tramped to a muddy quagmire by the horses tied to posts along the front of the buildings. They stood with their heads down and their backsides to the cutting gale.

Sioux and Cheyenne women huddled out of the

wind in the doorway of the storage building. He caught a glimpse of crates piled nearly to the ceiling through the open doorway. Trying to ignore the stench of so many unwashed bodies, he pushed his way into the smoke-filled room and looked around for someone in charge.

A scrawny, red-necked young man with stringy blond hair seemed to be directing the dispersal of crates. Impatience was etched around his mouth as he argued with a young Sioux brave. "We ain't giving out no ammunition. You can have some extra bean rations."

"Beans, bah! Must have gunpowder!" The Sioux warrior spat for emphasis at the young man's feet.

"Learn to grow crops like normal folk, and you wouldn't have to worry about shootin' buffalo. Now either take your rations and go, or get out of the way so the rest can get their grub."

The young brave scowled and swept the rations into the skirt the woman with him held ready. He gave the young man one last glare before stomping away.

Rand pushed his way up to the counter, and the man looked up. "Lieutenant Rand Campbell. I was ordered to see if there's anything you need. You are the new trader, aren't you?"

The young man licked his lips, and his eyes darted toward a door to the side of the counter. "No, sir. Name's Les Johnson and I just work for him. He's in his office right now with some folks. I'll tell him you stopped by, though."

"You do that. I have another errand to run. I'll stop back later this afternoon." Rand turned to leave and almost ran into a familiar lanky figure with dirty blond hair and pale blue eyes. "Labe?" Rand stared, almost not believing his own eyes, but it was definitely Labe Croftner. What was he doing here? His blood pounded in his ears, and he swallowed the lump of rage in his throat. "Where's Ben?" Labe would never roam this far from home without his brother.

"R-Rand!" Labe's eyes widened and he started to back away, but Rand grabbed his arm so tightly he flinched.

"Where is he?"

His face white, Labe shook his head, but his eyes darted to the closed door to the right of the counter. Rand released his arm and strode toward the door.

"Wait, you can't go in there!" Labe moved to intercept him, but Rand brushed by him and threw open the door.

Ben was seated at a makeshift desk with two rough-looking men dressed in buckskin sitting across from him on crates. His gray eyes widened when he saw Rand, then he smiled and stood, swiping his white-blond hair out of his face. "Well, well, well, if it isn't the illustrious Lieutenant Campbell come to pay me a call. I didn't expect word of my arrival to reach you quite this soon."

"What are you doing here, Croftner?" Rand clenched his fists and took a step toward the desk.

"What does it look like? I'm the new trader, old friend. This opportunity was too good to pass up, so I decided to put up with the disagreeable thought of having to run into you occasionally and took the job." Ben offered Rand an insolent smile and sat back down. "And a very lucrative one, too, I might add. Now if you don't mind, I have business to attend to."

Rand choked back his rage. He needed a clear head to deal with Croftner. There was some nefarious purpose to Ben's presence here, he was sure. "I'll be watching you, Croftner. You step out of line just one inch, and I'll be all over you like a wolf on a rabbit."

Ben smiled indolently. "I'm terrified. Can't you see me shake?" The other men guffawed, and he leaned forward. "Give Sarah my love, and tell her I'll stop and see her real soon."

Rand gritted his teeth. "You stay away from Sarah."

"My, my. Does your lovely fiancée know how you still feel about Sarah? Perhaps I should inform her how you're still looking after the poor little orphan." He sat back and crossed his muddy boot over his knee. "But the beautiful Jessica doesn't have anything to worry about. Sarah belongs to me, and she's going to discover that real soon."

"You lay one finger on Sarah, and you'll be in the guardhouse so fast you won't know what happened."

"Hey, there's no law against calling on a lady."

"She doesn't want to see you."

"I think I'll just let her tell me that. I'm sure she'd be pretty cut up about discovering her precious Rand is about to marry someone else."

Tired of the exchange, Rand clenched his jaw. This was getting him nowhere. He turned and stalked out the door as the men behind him burst into raucous laughter.

His jaw tight and his chest pounding, Rand swung up into the saddle. Ranger danced a bit, as if to ask what the trouble was. Rand patted his neck, then urged him down the trail back to the fort. Did Sarah know Ben would follow her out here? How much did she really care for Croftner? After all, she had agreed to marry him once.

When he arrived back at the fort, he marched over to see Sarah. She had her sleeves rolled up, and tendrils of hair had escaped her neat roll. A smudge of flour marred her flushed cheek, and she moved the loaf of rising dough out of the way.

He resisted the urge to reach out and wipe it off. "I got your slate."

She smiled and rubbed at the smudge of flour on her face. "Thanks for tending to it so quickly. I'm a little scared about it, Rand. What if I can't teach them? I don't know any Sioux words at all."

"You'll do fine, Sarah." He stuffed his hands in his pockets. "Heard from Ben lately?"

A frown crouched between her eyes. "No, and I don't expect to. I made my feelings about him very clear."

The tightness eased from his chest. "He's here, Sarah."

Her eyes widened. "Here? As in Fort Laramie?"

He nodded. "He's the new fur trader. He's crooked enough to make a good one."

She eyed him. "You've talked to him?"

"I think he came because you're here. He said to give you his love."

Her scarlet cheeks went white. "He was just trying to annoy you. He knows I never want to see him again."

Ben was just as full of lies as he'd always been. Rand resolved to alert the soldiers to keep an eye on Sarah and make sure Croftner didn't pull anything.

❧

The soldiers had shoveled paths through the snow to all the buildings. The wind skated across the tops of the drifts as Sarah and Joel set out for the chapel. Her pulse thumped in her neck, and she wished she could have gotten out of this assignment.

Joel carried the stacks of slate for her. She didn't want him to grow up uneducated, and he was curious about the Indian children. It was a good way to interest him in studies. As she approached the small chapel, a group of about thirty youngsters watched her advance. She noticed one older girl of about seventeen. She was truly beautiful, with soft, dark eyes, glossy black braids, and an eager look on her face.

The girl stepped forward as Sarah stopped in front of the door. "I am Morning Song, daughter of White Raven," she said softly. "I very glad to learn more English."

The yearning in the young woman's face touched Sarah. "You speak well already." She opened the door and led them inside. Someone had already started a fire in the stove, and the room was warm and welcoming. She motioned for the children to be seated and waited until the rustling stopped.

"I'm Miss Sarah." She didn't want them to have to start off with a difficult word like Montgomery. "Can you say Miss Sarah?"

Dark eyes stared at her solemnly, then Morning Song spoke sharply. In unison they said, "Miss Sarah."

Sarah smiled. "Very good. This is my brother Joel." Several of the youngsters had already been eyeing him. He smiled at them uncertainly. "Could you tell me the names of the children, Morning Song?"

The Indian girl stood and put a hand on the sleek head of each child as she spoke. "This Dark River. This Spotted Dove, this Spotted Buckskin Girl. She is daughter of Chief Spotted Tail. Her Sioux name is Ah-ho-appa."

Sarah smiled at the musical names. "How lovely."

The names went on and on. How would she keep them all straight? "You'll have to help me for a few days until I can memorize them."

Morning Song nodded eagerly. "I very much like to help, Miss Sarah."

The day went well, with the children all eager to learn. Sarah was surprised at how quickly they picked up the English words.

"That was fun." Joel's face shone with enthusiasm. "I even learned some Sioux."

⟡

Sarah was clattering around in the kitchen and Joel was out playing with Red Hawk when the front door banged open. "We're in the kitchen," Sarah called. She poured water from the wooden bucket into the kettle and set it on the stove as Rand came in.

Amelia rinsed the last of the breakfast dishes and dried her hands on her voluminous apron before untying it and draping it over the back of a chair. "I'm going to meet Jacob at the sutler's store. I'll be back for lunch." She smiled at Rand as she went out the door.

Sarah grabbed a coffee cup. "Want some coffee?"

"Yeah." He pulled out a chair and sat. "I wanted to hear about your first day of class."

She poured him a cup of coffee and handed it to him. "It was okay. Most of the little ones don't know any English, but there was an older teenager who speaks well. You'll get a chance to meet her if you stay a little while. Morning Song and Ah-ho-appa will be here anytime."

Rand curled his hands around his cup and frowned. "Be careful not to get too close to the Sioux, Sarah. You may be doing a lot of harm."

"Whatever do you mean? I would never hurt them."

"Maybe not intentionally. But have you thought about how they may become discontented with their lives as Sioux? If you give them too many different ideas, they may not fit in with their own people."

"That's ridiculous! Ah-ho-appa is a chief's daughter. Maybe she can help her people climb up out of the primitive way of life they lead." She jumped to her feet and took the steaming kettle off the stove. "You soldiers would have them stay in squalor. Rooster told Joel the only good Indian was a dead one!" She jerked her apron around her waist and tied it before she spun around to face him.

Rand sighed and ran his large hand through his hair. "A lot of the soldiers feel that way, but you surely don't believe I do. You know White Snake was one of my best friends back home." He and the Miami brave had been friends since Rand was five. "You're new out here, Sarah. There's a lot of prejudice and bitter feelings against Indians. You need to be careful about meddling in things you don't know anything about. I wish things were different. But I've seen too many Indian women taken advantage of in the short time I've been here. I wouldn't want anything to spoil Morning Song."

Sarah opened her mouth to defend herself, but there was a timid knock on the back door. She bit back the angry words and opened the door with a bright smile. She didn't want her friends to hear their discussion and think they shouldn't come back.

Morning Song peeked in the door, and Ah-ho-appa was behind her with timid, gentle eyes. Morning Song's black hair gleamed in the sunlight. Behind them Sarah heard Rand suck in his breath, presumably when he saw Morning Song's beauty.

"Miss Sarah, we are too early?" Morning Song dropped her gaze as Rand rose to his feet.

"I was just going. Think about what I said, Sarah."
He smiled at the young women and strode out the door.

"You're just in time, Morning Song, Ah-ho-appa.
The tea is ready." Sarah ignored Rand's departure. He
hadn't given her a chance to explain her intentions. She
wanted to show God's love to her Sioux friends. She
swallowed her anger and poured them all a cup of tea.

Ah-ho-appa ran a gentle brown hand around the
gold rim of Amelia's bone-thin china and sighed as she
took an eager sip.

"What do we do today, Miss Sarah?" Morning
Song asked.

"I thought we might go for a walk while the weather
holds. Some of the men are predicting more cold weather
within a few days, so we should take advantage of
the sunshine while we can. I thought we might walk by
the river."

Morning Song nodded. Her lovely face glowed
with such joy and zest for life Sarah found all her
angry thoughts fading away. She untied her apron and
hung it on the peg by the door, then went to fetch her
bonnet and cloak from the front hall.

The wind was a gentle whisper instead of its usual
gale force. Mountain chickadees chittered in the trees

along the riverbank, and the sound was soothing. The last few days had been unusually warm, above freezing for a change. Morning Song skipped along beside Sarah while Ah-ho-appa eagerly led the way. They passed several groups of soldiers felling trees for firewood, the heavy thunk of their axes comfortingly familiar.

For Sarah, it brought back memories of her father and brothers clearing the back pasture the summer before the war began. Those were happy days, days of laughter and contentment. In those days, Rand hurried over every evening after his work was done on the farm to take her for a buggy ride or just a walk by the river.

A small sigh escaped her, and Morning Song looked up, her face clouding. "Why are you so sad, Miss Sarah? Blue coat with holes in cheeks make you unhappy?"

Sarah smiled at her friend's reference to Rand's dimples. "How did you know that?"

"Your cheeks are red like an apple, and you look like this when I come in." Morning Song scowled. "Eyes sparkle like dew on leaf. Miss Sarah love blue coat?"

Sarah nodded. "Very much. But sometimes he makes me so mad."

"You marry blue coat?" Ah-ho-appa asked.

"I was engaged to him before the war, long before he ever met Jessica. But now he is going to marry Miss DuBois. Do you know what engaged is?"

Ah-ho-appa nodded. "Promised to marry. My mother wishes me to promise myself to Red Fox, but I say no. I want to marry blue coat and live in fine house like Miss Sarah's."

Sarah looked at her in dismay. "Oh, Ah-ho-appa, you don't mean that. It would be best for you to marry one of your own people."

"You think I am not good enough for blue coat?"

"You're a treasure, Ah-ho-appa. Any man would be lucky to have you. But it's complicated . . . You don't understand how hard it would be for you with a white man."

"My friend River Flower marry blue coat and live at edge of fort. She have baby boy."

Sarah knew she referred to the common-law marriage where the soldier paid the girl's father a few horses and "married" her. When he moved on to another fort, he generally left his woman and any children behind. "You deserve more than that. Those marriages aren't legal in the sight of the white man's laws. You should look for a man who will love and take care of you always."

Ah-ho-appa shook her head, her face set with determination. "I marry blue coat or no one." She turned and started back toward the cabin with Sarah trailing behind.

Morning Song looked at Sarah sadly. "I did not know Miss Sarah does not like our people." She turned and walked stiffly back toward the Indian encampment.

Sarah's heart sank as she followed the girl's erect figure. What had she done? And how was she going to fix it?

SEVEN

S miling officers were decked out in their dress uni-
forms, their brass buttons and black boots shining.
When Sarah arrived to the dance, she and Amelia were
claimed for dances immediately. As an awkward lieutenant whirled her around the dance floor, Sarah found her
gaze straying to Rand's dark head in the throng. He was
so tall, he was easy to spot. His chin rested on Jessica's
gleaming red head, and she was snuggled close to him.
Sarah dragged her eyes away and forced herself to make
polite conversation with poor Lieutenant Richards.

The evening became a blur as one officer after another claimed her for a dance. Would Rand ask her to dance? Such a foolish hope. Jessica wouldn't allow him out of her sight, she was sure. She danced twice with Isaac, Rand's bunky, then whirled on to the next soldier.

When there were only two more dances left, Jessica's father insisted on a dance with his daughter. Rand glanced Sarah's way, then made his way determinedly through the throng.

"Are you promised for this dance?" His voice was too polite.

"Not really. I don't think Joel will mind if he doesn't have to dance. I told him he had to dance with me so he could begin to learn. But his lesson will wait." She slid into his arms, and he guided her onto the floor.

She eyed his tense face. "You were right."

"About what?"

"Ah-ho-appa wants to marry a soldier and live in a home like mine. When I objected, she and Morning Song both thought I didn't think they were good enough to marry a white."

He nodded. "I'd heard Ah-ho-appa refused her father's choice for her. But don't beat yourself up over it. It may have happened anyway. There are a lot of Indian women who jump at the chance to take a soldier. And their families are well paid for them."

"That's awful!"

"I know, but it's the way things are out here. A woman doesn't have much value. Although as pretty as your friends are, they'll probably fetch a high price." His mouth twisted with distaste. "That will be a strong incentive to their fathers."

"Isn't there anything we can do?" Sarah couldn't stand the thought of her young friends sinking into that kind of life.

"Not really. Just be a friend to them. It's probably too late to do anything else."

The dance ended, and Rand escorted her to her chair. He stared down at her with a curious look on his face. It seemed almost tender. He opened his mouth but was interrupted by Jessica's arrival.

"There you are, darling," she cooed. "Be a dear and fetch me some punch."

"Of course. Would you care for some, Sarah?"

"No, thank you." She tensed as he walked away.

As soon as he was out of earshot, Jessica turned to her furiously. "Just what do you think you're going to accomplish by staying here? Why don't you just go home?"

Sarah forced a smile. "Jessica, we're just friends. And I'd like to be your friend too."

Confusion spread over Jessica's face, and she shook her head. "I have all the friends I need."

What more was there to say? "Very well."

Isaac Liddle approached the two women. "There's only one dance left." He extended his arm to Sarah. "May I?"

Rand was heading back, and the last thing she wanted was to be a hanger-on. She put her hand on his arm. "I'd be delighted."

He grinned down at her. "I know this might sound abrupt, Miss Sarah, but I figured I might as well throw my hat in the ring. With your permission, I'd really like to call on you."

Sarah hid her surprise. She'd seen Isaac hovering close over the past few weeks, but she had thought he was just being kind because he knew how hurt she'd been. "I don't know, Isaac. You're a good friend, and I'd hate to ruin our friendship."

"How could we ruin it? We could become even better friends."

Sarah was tempted. Isaac was a good Christian man and she had a lot of respect for him. "All right. But I can't make any promises."

He nodded. "I understand. Let's just get to know each other better and take it from there."

The next morning, Ah-ho-appa was absent from school, and Morning Song refused to even look at Sarah. Sarah's heart ached as she saw the stiffness in her friend's demeanor. Everything seemed such a hopeless tangle.

"Don't go, Morning Song," she said as the Indian girl stood to go home. "I want to talk to you."

The girl almost seemed like her old self as she nodded and motioned her brother to go on without her.

"You seem to be avoiding me. I can't stand for you to be upset with me. Won't you please forgive me if I hurt you when we talked last? I really didn't mean I didn't think you were good enough for a soldier. Any man would be very lucky to marry you or Ah-ho-appa."

"I was very angry, but no more. I know you not wish to hurt me. And I have new friend."

Sarah's heart sank at the glow on the girl's lovely face. "A man?"

The girl nodded. "He is very handsome. Very light hair with eyes like a stormy sky."

Sarah tried to think of a soldier who fit that description, but she couldn't think of who it might be. "What's his name?"

"He is the new fur trader. Ben Croftner." Morning Song smiled a secret smile as she said his name.

Sarah stepped back as from a blow. "Oh, Morning Song. Not Ben. He's a very wicked, evil man." She caught the girl's arm. "Please, please stay away from him!"

Morning Song shook her hand off. "He told me you will say this. But he loves me. He is a good man. He offered my father five horses for me. We will marry tomorrow."

"Please, Morning Song. I beg you. Don't do this. It isn't a legal marriage. Ben won't stay with you."

The girl just gave her an angry stare and stalked off. "I thought my friend be happy for me, but I was wrong," she called back over her shoulder. "You are my friend no more."

Sarah clasped her hands and paced the floor. What

could she do? She couldn't just stand back and let Morning Song make a mistake like that. She caught up her cloak and hurried to the door. There just might be one hope.

She had borrowed a horse from the stables and found the trail leading to the trading post across the river. Isaac was crossing the parade ground, so she had asked him to escort her. He commandeered a private, and the two soldiers rode with her across the river.

The trading post was almost deserted when she arrived. A few Sioux hunkered around a fire in the front and looked up as they rode into the yard.

She slid off her horse and handed her reins to Isaac. "Wait for me here if you would."

He frowned. "I'm not sure you should go in alone."

"I'll be fine. He knows you're out here."

Labe was just coming out the door as she approached the building. "Sarah! What are you doing here?"

"I'd hoped you hadn't followed Ben out here, Labe. I need to see him. Is he here?"

He nodded. "He's in his office. I'll show you." He opened the door and led her across the dirt floor to a battered door. He rapped on it once, then swung it open for her.

Ben looked up when he heard the door open. "Sarah?" He rose to his feet eagerly, but his smile faded. His expression masked, he motioned for her to sit on the crate across from his crude table. "To what do I owe the honor of this call?"

"I want you to leave Morning Song alone." She didn't have time for any pleasantries, even if she was inclined to offer them, which she wasn't. "We both know you don't really care about her. She's too sweet for you to ruin."

He stroked his chin. "She'll be a lovely addition to my home, don't you think? And Indian women really know how to treat a man. I just don't see how I can agree with your request."

"Please, Ben. Don't do this." She leaned forward. "I can't bear to see her hurt."

"You're begging now, are you? Well, I might agree under one condition." He smiled gently. "You could take her place."

Sarah flushed. She should have known he'd suggest something like this. "You know how I feel about you."

He stood and thrust his hands into his pockets. "You're just angry, and I'm not saying you don't have a right to be. But anything I did was only because I loved you. And you haven't had any luck with Rand, now have you?"

"Maybe not, but I couldn't marry a man I couldn't trust." Sarah stood. There was no more to say. She loved Morning Song, but it was out of her hands.

"Then the wedding proceeds tomorrow as planned."

"You know it's not a real wedding! You'll just send her back to her family when you're tired of her."

Ben sneered. "She's just a savage, Sarah. That's all Indian women are good for."

"She's sweet and good. You'll take that and destroy it!"

"My, my, you do have an exalted opinion of me, don't you? Well, you just run on back to your precious Rand and let me take care of my own affairs. But don't think this is the last of our discussion." He caught her by the wrist and pulled her into a tight embrace. She fought to get away, but he pulled her closer and tipped her chin up. "I mean to have you, Sarah. One way or the other. Things will never be over between us."

When he released her, she dashed for the door. Isaac had dismounted. His gaze searched hers, and his lips tightened. "Did he hurt you?"

Her eyes burned, but she shook her head. "Let's go home."

The next day Sarah watched the parade ground from the window as Ben arrived with five horses to take possession of his bride. In a beautifully beaded dress bleached to a pale yellow, Morning Song was seated on a horse almost the color of her dress. Her unbound hair, rippling past her waist, gleamed in the weak sunshine as she followed her new husband out of the fort. Sarah wept as she saw her friend's glowing face look back one last time.

The next day the weather made one of its drastic changes. The temperature plummeted, and the wind picked up. Then the blizzard Rooster had predicted struck in all its fury. The wind howled and blew snow through cracks around the windows. They all had to fight to keep the fires going in the fireplace. Jacob finally gave up the fight in the bedroom and dragged the bed and their belongings out into the kitchen.

They hung blankets over the doorway into the hall to try to block the flow of cold air. By the time the storm had vented its full fury, there were drifts of snow over the windows. Jacob opened the door only to be met with a column of snow completely covering the opening. They were effectively buried until the enlisted men dug them out. Sarah spent the day making loaves of bread while Amelia worked on a quilt. It was evening before they heard the scraping of shovels and friendly hellos from outside the door.

Sarah stood beside Jacob as he opened the door and two half-frozen men stumbled inside, their faces, beards, hair, and clothing all packed with snow.

"Glad to see you all are all right," the youngest private sputtered as he complied with Sarah's urging and took off his coat before staggering toward the fire. "The colonel said to tell you to stay inside tonight. We got a path dug out pert near all around the post so we can get from building to building. And the wood detail will be here with a load soon."

Amelia poured them all a cup of hot coffee and offered them bread and jam, which they accepted with alacrity. "Much obliged, ma'am." The young private got to his feet when the last crumb of bread was devoured. "We best be heading back to check with the colonel."

They saw their deliverers to the door and peered

out the narrow path left by their busy shovels. "It looks like a maze," Sarah said, unable to believe what she saw. The snow towered over twelve feet in many places. The narrow path trailed down the steps and around the corner toward Old Bedlam.

Jacob saw her shivering and shut the door. "You girls had better stay in until the weather breaks. Feels like it's at least twenty below. Exposed skin freezes in seconds in this kind of temperature."

※

The weather didn't break for days. There would be a couple of days of bright sunshine, but the temperatures were way below zero, and the wind howled and blew the snow into ever-changing drifts. Those days would be followed by more snow and yet more snow. Sarah and Amelia took to pacing around the tiny quarters when Jacob and Rand were gone on duty. Jacob was sent out on telegraph duty several times, he was officer of the day three times, and he took his turn guarding the cattle and horse herds. They all tried to keep busy. Sarah played endless games of checkers with Joel and Amelia while Jacob and Rand saw to their duties.

Mail hadn't been able to get through either. Sarah longed for news from home. Surely Rachel had delivered the baby by now.

Jacob kept them informed of the goings-on at the post. Big Ribs had returned with the Corn band of Brulé ready to make peace. Then Man-Afraid-of-His-Horses trudged in with his band of Oglala. The winter had been hard on all of them.

Sarah was forced to discontinue the lessons with the Indian children. The weather was too cold for the little ones to be out, but she intended to start again in the spring. Her thoughts turned often to Morning Song. How was Ben treating her? She continued her lessons with Joel, in spite of his protests. But no amount of activity could distract her long from her worry about her friend.

EIGHT

The weather finally broke and with its usual capriciousness turned unseasonably balmy. Sarah slid a plate of eggs in front of Jacob. "I heard you tell Amelia you were going to the trading post today. Could I come along? I want to visit Morning Song."

He hesitated, then nodded. "I'll have to take a couple more men along for protection. Make sure you dress warm."

She hurried to do his bidding. About an hour later, she hurried across the open parade ground toward the stable. Jacob and Isaac, along with five other soldiers, were waiting with a mount for her, and they set off for the Indian encampment around the trading post.

The little settlement was full of Indians and trappers when they arrived. Sioux women stood around smoky fires patiently, but Sarah didn't see her friend. Isaac pointed out Ben's cabin, set off in a grove of trees by itself.

"I'll keep Ben busy," he promised.

Sarah dismounted and hurried toward the cabin. No one answered her first knock, so she rapped harder. Finally the door opened, and Morning Song peered around the door.

"Sarah," she gasped. She started to shut the door, but Sarah saw the marks on her face and pushed her way in.

"Oh, Morning Song," was all she could say for a moment. The young woman's face was marred by ugly purple and yellow bruises. One eye was swollen almost shut, and her lips were split and puffy. Morning Song cried softly as Sarah took her in her arms.

Morning Song pulled away and wiped at her eyes gingerly with the hem of her apron. "Do not look at me."

Sarah brushed the hair out of her friend's face.

"Why have you stayed? Didn't you know I would take you in?"

Morning Song lifted her hands, palms upward. "Ben is always watching me. He says if I leave, he will make me sorry. He says he will hurt you."

Sarah gathered the young woman back into her arms. "Don't you worry about Ben. He can't hurt me. The blue coats won't let him." She released her. "Get your buffalo robe and any possessions you want. You're coming with me."

When Morning Song was ready, Sarah opened the door cautiously and looked around. No one seemed to be paying any attention to the little cabin. "You stay in the trees. We'll meet you just over the knoll."

Morning Song nodded and slipped away sound-lessly. Sarah hurried along the path and quickly mounted her horse. She told one of the soldiers to wait for Jacob while she took the others and started for home. Her heart pounded. If Ben looked out and saw her, he'd know for sure that something was up. She looked back as she rounded the bend. There was no hue and cry, so she began to breathe easier.

When she crested the knoll, she heard a scuffle and a cry to her right. "Morning Song," she called.

She urged her horse through the frozen brush with the soldiers following her. As she crashed through the thicket, she saw Morning Song struggling with a man. "Let go of her, Labe."

He looked up, his eyes startled. "Ben will have my hide," he whined. "I'm s'posed to see she doesn't get away. It's nothing to you, Sarah."

"Look at her, Labe. Go on. Look at her. Do you honestly think Ben has a right to beat her like that?"

Labe glanced at the Indian girl's battered face and dropped his eyes. "You know how Ben can be."

"I know. Now let go of her."

Labe's hand fell away, and Morning Song picked up her bundle and scurried toward Sarah. Sarah reached out a hand and helped her swing up on the back of her horse.

"Ben's going to be mad."

"You tell him to stay away from me and Morning Song." She nodded to the privates who had followed her, and they all crashed back through the thicket to the trail.

Isaac and the detachment were just rounding the crest of the knoll as they arrived. Isaac whistled when he saw Morning Song's face. "Ben do that?"

Sarah nodded, her lips tight. "Thanks for keeping him busy."

"No problem. We'd better hurry, though. He'll be after us any minute. He said something about going home for lunch. As soon as he sees she's missing, he's going to be hunting for her."

"He'll know where to look. Labe saw us." She quickly told him and Jacob the full story as they kicked their horses and galloped toward the safety of the fort.

When they reached the fort, Morning Song insisted on going to the Indian encampment. "I must see my father. He will wish to know."

Sarah and Jacob exchanged a long look. This could cause a major incident.

∼⟫⟪∼

Sarah helped Amelia hang up clothes on a line strung around the living room. The scent of lye soap stung her eyes, and she rubbed her reddened hands in the folds of her skirt. "I think I should go check on Morning Song. She should have been back by now. What if Ben waylaid her?"

"Jacob had a couple of soldiers watching. I don't

think he could get her." Amelia put on her cloak. "I'm going to the sutler's store for a few things. Want to come?"

She shook her head. "I want to wait here for Morning Song."

With the house empty, she paced the floor and waited. The cannon boomed as the soldiers went through the flag-lowering ritual. Maybe Ben was going to let Morning Song leave without protest.

Then a fist came down on the front door so hard that a picture on the wall by the door fell to the floor. Ben bellowed from the other side. Sarah picked up the picture. She just wouldn't answer. Maybe he'd go away. Her gaze went to the doorknob. She didn't remember locking it after Amelia left.

She looked around for a weapon, but nothing was in sight.

"Where is she?" he shouted.

Sarah bit her lip and said nothing. The doorknob began to turn, and she caught her breath as the door opened. Cold air rushed into the parlor, then Ben burst inside.

Sarah took a step back. "Get out of here, Ben. How dare you show your face here after what you did to Morning Song?"

His face reddened. "She is my property. No one complains if I discipline my horse, now do they? This is none of your business." He strode across the floor and caught her by the arms before she could even flinch away. He took her chin and tilted her head up as she struggled to get away. "I like it when you fight me," he whispered.

She stopped her struggling instantly, and he laughed again before releasing her. "Run away, little rabbit. But you won't escape me. I have plans for you."

Her pulse jumped in her throat. He was terrifying.

He leered at her, then stomped back out the door. "I'll find her, Sarah. She'll wish she'd stayed where she belonged. And you'll wish you'd stayed out of it."

Sarah let out a shaky breath as the door banged behind him. How had she ever thought he was attractive and kind? She shuddered. The door burst open again, and she flinched. But it was Rand.

"Are you all right?"

She nodded, close to tears. She hated to admit it, even to herself, but she was afraid of Ben. He was truly mad. "He's l-looking for Morning Song," she stammered, then burst into tears.

Rand crossed the room in one stride and pulled her into his arms. "It's all right, Green Eyes. We won't let him take her." He caressed her hair until the storm of weeping was past.

"I'm sorry," she gulped. "I don't know what came over me." She was very aware of his hand on her hair. That hand tightened on the back of her neck when she looked up.

Rand swallowed hard when she put a hand on his cheek. She searched his face and saw confusion mixed with a tenderness she'd hoped to find for weeks. "Rand," she began. But the door opened and Amelia rushed in. She'd heard the story at Suds Row.

Rand stepped away quickly, and the moment was lost. Again.

A JOURNEY *of the* HEART

AVAILABLE IN PRINT STARTING MARCH 2015

THOMAS NELSON
Since 1798

A vacation to Sunset Cove was her way of
celebrating and thanking her parents. After all,
Claire Dellamore's childhood was like a fairytale.
But with the help of Luke Elwell, Claire discovers
that fairytale was really an elaborate lie . . .

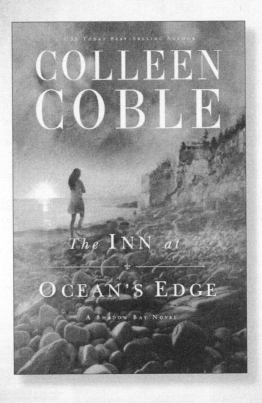

The first Sunset Cove Novel

Available April 2015

Thomas Nelson
Since 1798

9780718001759-B

COLLEEN LOVES TO HEAR FROM HER READERS!

Be sure to sign up for Colleen's newsletter for insider information on deals and appearances.

Visit her website at www.colleencoble.com
Twitter: @colleencoble
Facebook: colleencoblebooks

THOMAS NELSON
Since 1798

ABOUT THE AUTHOR

Photo by Clik Chick Photography

R ITA finalist Colleen Coble is the author of several
bestselling romantic suspense novels, including
Tidewater Inn, and the Mercy Falls, Lonestar, and
Rock Harbor series.